Safari Guide!
Scouting for Wildlife in Africa

Written by Robyn Brode

Photography by Todd Wayne

Illustrated by Paul Hayes

BARRON'S

First edition for the United States and Canada published exclusively by Barron's Educational Series, Inc. in 2002

Created and produced by Orange Avenue Publishing, Inc., San Francisco
© 2002 Orange Avenue Publishing, Inc.
Illustrations © 2002 Paul Hayes
Photographs © 2002 Todd Wayne

All inquiries should be addressed to:
Barron's Educational Series, Inc.
250 Wireless Boulevard
Hauppauge, NY 11788
http://www.barronseduc.com

International Standard Book No. 0-7641-2152-9

Library of Congress Catalog Card No. 2001097896

Printed in Singapore
9 8 7 6 5 4 3 2 1

Safari Guide!

Scouting for Wildlife in Africa

AFRICA

This map of Africa highlights three countries that have many game parks. Shown below are their colorful flags.

Kenya

Tanzania

Zimbabwe

My uncle is a safari guide. He
drives people in his jeep into an
African game park, so they can
see the wildlife that lives there.

Today, my uncle is taking me on my own safari. We climb into the jeep, and get to the game park just as the sun is rising.

Right away, we see some buffalo.
They seem to be in a hurry.
Maybe they like to travel while
it's still cool.

There are no roads here, just land as far as we can see. Lots of animals are grazing on the flat, grassy plain.

We pass a herd of elephants.
It's hard to believe they spend
sixteen hours a day eating,
mostly leaves from trees.

We see an impala grazing
in the grass. It looks up as
we drive by.

DID YOU KNOW?
In a herd, zebras' stripes create a confusing pattern, making it difficult for predators to pick out a single zebra.

In the distance, we see a group of zebras. My uncle hands me the binoculars, so I can get a close-up view.

Suddenly a lioness and her cub walk out of their hiding places in the tall grass.

The lioness watches us closely as we pass by. She wants to make sure we don't hurt her cub!

We hear many birdcalls coming from the trees. Most of them are hard to spot. But not the eagle, sitting by its nest.

Then my uncle points out a yellow-billed hornbill, just taking off from a tree branch.

We've been driving and looking
at wildlife all morning. It's time
to stop and eat lunch.

DID YOU KNOW?

Giraffes have seven bones in their necks, just like humans do. But the bones are larger, so they make a m-u-c-h longer neck.

For a change, we are the ones being watched. This giraffe has decided to have lunch with us.

DID YOU KNOW?

Hippos eat only after the sun goes down. They can eat about 90 pounds of grass in one night. That's a lot!

Now that we're rested and full, we're ready to go again. As we drive on, we see a hippo sitting in a mud hole.

I learn that hippos spend their days in mud or water to keep cool. I'm so hot, I wish I had a water hole to jump into!

Now we see some animals
jumping around on two feet
in the tall grass. My uncle says
they're Chackma baboons.

We try to count them — there are four or five hiding in the grass. There's another one in a tree.

It is late in the afternoon when we start back. We have a long way to go before we leave the game park.

We stop to look again and again as we drive. I think about all the wild animals and birds we have seen, just in one day.

The sun is beginning to sink.
We watch in silence as the sky
becomes full of brilliant colors.
It is an awesome sight.

We reach the edge of the
game park just as night falls.
We have had a long, full day
and are ready to go home.

Tonight, curled up in my bed,
my head is filled with the sights
and sounds of all I saw today.

I fall asleep thinking that one day perhaps I'll be a safari guide, scouting for wildlife in Africa.

RIAL GUINEA

GA

In the game parks of Africa, many kinds of animals live in the wild. They also live wildly!

The animals that live in game parks are safe. No one can harm them or take them away.

Humans are welcome to come for a visit. But they can only watch as the animals go about their daily lives.

Wild animals find their own food and water, and choose where they sleep.

Monkeys eat leaves and live in trees.

Zebras eat grass on the plains and lie down where the grass grows tall.

Lions eat meat and rest near bushes.

Giraffes eat leaves high up in trees and sleep on the ground nearby.

ZAIRE

UGANDA

KENYA

SOMALIA

RWANDA

BURUNDI

TANZANIA

NGO

NGOLA

ZAMBIA

MOZAMBIQUE

ZIMBABWE

AMIBIA

BOTSWANA

SWAZILAND

LESOTHO

SOUTH
AFRICA

DID YOU KNOW?

Africa is a huge continent, and its many countries have millions of miles of land set aside for wildlife to roam free.

GLOSSARY

A safari is a guided wilderness trip to see wildlife. Hunters used to go on African safaris to shoot wild animals. Now people just "shoot" pictures, and they "go on safari" by driving around in game parks.

Game means animals that are hunted for sport or for food. The huge parks in Africa set aside for wildlife are called game parks because, in the past, wild animals were hunted.

When animals eat grass and other small plants, they are grazing. There is plenty of greenery to eat all year long on the plains of Africa.

A plain is an expanse of land that is mostly flat and has few trees. A plain can be low like a valley or high and flat like a plateau, but you can always see a long way in every direction.

A herd of large animals refers to a group of the same kind of animals that stays together.

In the wild, some animals eat vegetables like grass or leaves. Others like to eat insects. Predators are animals that eat meat. They prey on other animals and try to kill them for food.

A binocular is a small telescope. Put two of them together and you have a pair of binoculars. When you look through binoculars, things seem very close, even though they are far away.

A lioness is a mother lion, and a cub is a baby lion. The father is just called a lion.

Birdcalls are the notes and cries that birds make. A series of birdcalls makes a bird song. You can recognize different kinds of birds by their calls and songs.

The books in the **Going Places** series
are produced by Orange Avenue, Inc.

Creative Director: **Hallie Warshaw**
Writer: **Robyn Brode** • Designer: **Britt Menendez**
Illustrator: **Paul Hayes** • Coordinator and
researcher: **Emily Vassos**
Photos: **Todd Wayne** and **Eyewire**

Original concept for series:
Hallie Warshaw and
Mark Shulman